D0987988

ʳned to any branch of the
or before ᵗʰᵉ ᵈᵃ

Lancashire Library Services	
12378728	
PETERS	JF
£4.99	29-May-2012

KING SOLOMON'S MINES

Adapted by Russell Punter

Illustrated by Matteo Pincelli

Reading consultant: Alison Kelly
University of Roehampton

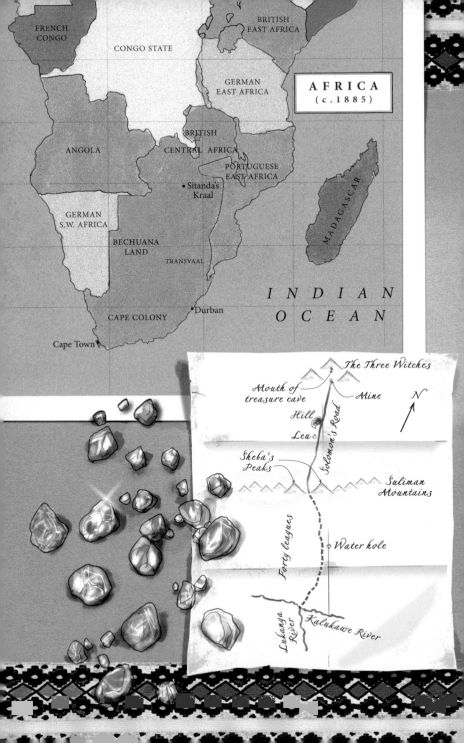

FRENCH
CONGO

CONGO STATE

BRITISH
EAST AFRICA

GERMAN
EAST AFRICA

AFRICA
(c.1885)

ANGOLA

BRITISH
CENTRAL AFRICA

PORTUGUESE
EAST AFRICA

• Sitanda's
Kraal

MADAGASCAR

GERMAN
S.W. AFRICA

BECHUANA
LAND

TRANSVAAL

I N D I A N

O C E A N

CAPE COLONY

• Durban

Cape Town •

The Three Witches

Mouth of
treasure cave

Mine

N

Hill

Leu

Solomon's Road

Sheba's
Peaks

Suliman
Mountains

Water hole

Forty leagues

Lukanga
River

Kalukawe River

Contents

Chapter 1

Lost in Africa

The most extraordinary adventure of my life began aboard a steamship sailing from Cape Town to Durban.

I had experienced many dangers during my time in Africa. But, as I strolled around the deck on that cool January night, little could have prepared me for the nerve-shattering perils that lay ahead.

"Excuse me, sir," came a booming voice behind me. I turned to see a great bear of a man, broad-chested, with flowing golden hair and a fullsome beard. "But are you by any chance Mr. Allan Quatermain?" he asked.

"I am," I replied, cautiously.

The fellow seemed relieved. "My name is Sir Henry Curtis," he declared with a smile. "And this is my friend, Captain John Good." He gestured to a shorter, stout man beside him, who wore a monocle in his right eye that sparkled in the twilight.

"When I discovered you were on board, I had to speak with you," said Sir Henry. "If you'd be kind enough to dine with us this evening, I'll explain everything."

Over dinner, Sir Henry told me that he had come all the way from England in search of his brother.

"Three years ago, my brother and I argued, Mr. Quatermain. I needn't trouble you with the details, save that it ended with George setting off to southern Africa to make his fortune."

"Sir Henry has neither seen nor heard from him since," added Captain Good.

"I'm determined to bring my brother home and make amends," said Sir Henry.

"You have quite a reputation in this part of the world, Mr. Quatermain," said Good. "Our inquiries have led us to believe that you may have met Sir Henry's brother."

"Two years ago, when you were trading in the Transvaal?" prompted Sir Henry, eagerly.

I cast my mind back. "It's some time ago, gentlemen. Even so, I don't recall ever meeting a George Curtis..."

"We believe he was calling himself Neville at the time," interjected Good.

Something about this name struck a chord. "Yes, there was a fellow," I recalled. "He camped nearby for two weeks or so."

Sir Henry could hardly contain his excitement. "And what became of him, Mr. Quatermain? Did he tell you where he was headed?"

"Oh yes, gentlemen," I replied solemnly. The memory was only too clear now. "He was searching for King Solomon's Mines."

Chapter 2

The legend of the mines

"I first heard the legend of King Solomon's Mines about thirty years ago, from an old elephant hunter," I explained. "They are said to date back over two thousand years, and lie somewhere north of the Suliman Mountains."

"What was mined there?" asked Good.

"Diamonds, Captain," I replied. "More diamonds than any man has seen before or since – so the legend says."

"You don't believe it, then?" said Sir Henry.

"I might not have done, were it not for an incident some twenty years back. I was out at Sitanda's Kraal, just north of the Lukanga River. One day, a Portuguese fellow by the name of Silvestre staggered into my camp.

He'd come from the direction of the desert and was nothing but skin and bone."

Sir Henry looked aghast. "What had happened to the poor devil?" he asked.

"He'd tried to cross the desert and ran out of water," I replied, shuddering at the memory of that wretched figure. "Before he died, he handed me a map."

I took a sheet of paper from my pocket-book. "This is my translation of the original."

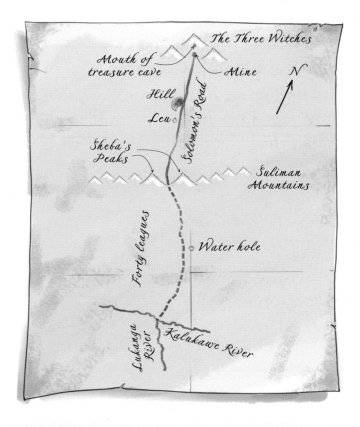

"Silvestre said the map was made by one of his ancestors," I went on. "This relative had made it to the mines, but died on the return journey, empty handed save for the map."

"So Sir Henry's brother was on the same mission as these Silvestres," sighed Good.

"It needn't mean that George has met with a similar fate," said Sir Henry.

"Before your brother set off, I gave his servant a note with the directions mentioned on the map," I explained. "That may have given him a chance."

Sir Henry shot Good a determined look. "Then we must go after George," he declared, "to King Solomon's Mines."

Good frowned. "We'll need a guide."

Sir Henry fixed me with a steely gaze. "Mr. Quatermain," he said, "will you join us?"

Chapter 3

The desert of danger

So it was, that, five months later, our party arrived at Sitanda's Kraal. It had been a thousand mile journey from Durban, the last three hundred on foot, due to deadly tsetse flies that had killed our oxen.

On the way, I managed to teach Sir Henry and Good some Zulu, and they had both become fairly proficient.

We had been joined on our mission by two servants I'd hired at Durban – a tough little bushman I knew named Ventvögel, and Umbopa, a tall, handsome-looking Zulu, a stranger to me, who'd offered his services quite out of the blue.

11

After a brief rest, we left Sitanda's Kraal and began our trek across the desert.

We decided to travel by night and rest by day, so as to reduce exposure to the scorching desert sun. The first daylight stop passed well enough, though I was glad of the large gourds of water we carried with us. We spent the time sleeping beneath the shade of a massive boulder, and by late afternoon we set off again.

By dawn the next day, we were ready to drop, but no sizeable shade presented itself.

Then Good had the notion of digging a pit and burying ourselves inside. It seemed worth a try, but even with sprigs cut from nearby karoo bushes to cover us, we could only withstand the discomfort for a few hours.

Slowly we trudged on and on, until we had covered some forty-five miles.

"Only another fifteen miles and we should reach the water hole on Silvestre's map," I gasped, my lips as parched as dry leaves.

But it seemed that luck was not on our side. At the spot where the water hole should have been, there was nothing but a massive sand hill. We slumped down despondently in the shade it offered, and sipped down our last few pathetic drops of liquid from the gourds.

As we slipped into unconsciousness, Umbopa spoke what we all feared. "If we can't find water, we shall all be dead before the moon rises tomorrow."

Chapter 4

Tragedy on the mountain

We slept as best we could, before waking with our torturous thirsts still raging. It was then that Ventvögel became agitated, pointing at a row of animal tracks in the sand.

"Springboks don't go far from water," he said, excitedly sniffing the air. "I can smell it, Mr. Quatermain."

I couldn't see how. "There's not a drop of water in sight," I argued.

Sir Henry stroked his long beard thoughtfully. "Perhaps it's on *top* of the hill, Quatermain?" he suggested, looking upwards.

The idea hardly seemed credible, but we were too desperate to discount it. We scrambled up the sandy side of the mound until we reached the summit.

There, sure enough, was a small pool of water. How it came to be there I will never know, but thank heaven for it. We joyously drank, bathed and filled our water gourds. Then, as night fell, we set off once more, our spirits restored.

Ahead of us, we could make out the two enormous, snow-capped mountains that were Sheba's Peaks. Forty-eight hours later, we found ourselves on their lower slopes.

It soon became clear that these mighty peaks must once have been volcanoes. The ground beneath our feet was hardened lava now, which made the ascent a painful one.

As we got higher up, the air became cooler and cooler. At first, this came as a relief after the baking heat of the desert. But as we began to encounter patches of snow, we realized that we had merely exchanged one danger for another. Within a couple of days, the temperature had dropped to something like ten or fifteen degrees below zero. By now, our rations of dried meat were gone, and it seemed like we had escaped death by thirst only to die of hunger.

As dusk approached one night, Umbopa grabbed Good's arm and pointed to what appeared to be a hole in the snow. "A cave!" he cried.

We piled into the tiny cavern and huddled together for warmth. We sat for hour after hour through that bitter night, the frost eating into our miserable, starved carcasses.

Ventvögel's back was pressed against mine, and as the night wore on, it seemed to get colder and colder, till at last it was like ice.

The next morning, as the sun's rays reached the mouth of the cave, they illuminated a terrible sight. There sat the poor fellow, totally immobile, frozen to death.

Our spirits were laid low after this tragic loss. But we had no choice but to leave our loyal friend to his eternal vigil, and set off once again on our mission.

We hadn't gone more than half a mile when, some five hundred yards beneath us, at the end of a long slope of snow, we saw a patch of green grass, through which a stream was running. By the stream stood a group of antelopes, basking in the morning sun. A short while later, we were enjoying our first fresh meat for many days.

As we descended further, the mountain mist began to lift to reveal a wonderful sight.

There, some five thousand feet or so below, stretched mile after mile of greenery. The landscape lay before us like a map, patches of forest here, rich undulating grassland there, broken by a glistening blue river. In the distance, we could just make out herds of game or cattle, and groups of dome-shaped huts.

"Look!" cried Sir Henry, pointing at a wide, white path to our right that led from the mountain and sliced its way through the countryside. "Remember Silvestre's map – that must be Solomon's Road!"

Chapter 5

Kingdom of the Kukuanas

We followed the curious man-made path as it snaked its way down the mountainside to the valley below.

It wasn't long before we left the mountain altogether and continued our journey through a wooded landscape, through which a brook babbled along merrily. The whole place was like paradise on Earth.

We decided to stop to take a much needed bath, and were engrossed in our preparations, when a flash of light whizzed past Good's head.

Turning, I saw a group of tall, copper-skinned men, dressed in leopard skin cloaks and plumes of white feathers. At their head was a muscular boy of seventeen or so.

He was crouched in the pose of a warrior who has just unleashed a weapon. Sure enough, embedded in a tree, a few feet from us, was a large knife.

The youth lunged toward us, but was held in check by an elderly warrior.

"I am Infadoos," declared this man, in a tongue so similar to Zulu it was simple to understand. "And this is Scragga," he said, pointing at the scowling boy, "son of King Twala – Twala the one-eyed, the wicked, the terrible."

"Like father, like son," complained Good under his breath.

"Where have you come from?" demanded Infadoos. "And what are you?" he added, clearly mystified by the pale skin of most of our party.

"We come in peace from beyond the mountains," I replied.

"You lie," said Scragga. "No man can cross the mountains where all things perish. But whoever you are, no strangers may live in the land of the Kukuanas. It's the King's law. Prepare to die!"

As one, the men surrounded us and raised the fearsome-looking spears they were carrying.

"Wait!" I cried, gesturing to Umbopa to hand me one of the rifles. "We come from another world, from the biggest star that shines at night. I'll prove it to you."

I pointed to an antelope grazing about seventy yards away. "Can an ordinary man bring down a beast from here with just a noise?" I asked.

"It isn't possible," replied Infadoos.

I took aim, fired, and, accompanied by a loud crack from my weapon, the antelope fell to earth. A gasp arose from the Kukuanas.

"These are wizards indeed," said the elderly warrior, who had clearly never seen any type of firearm before. "They must meet the King."

"Lead us then, to Twala," I cried.

"And also, let's hope, to my brother," added Sir Henry.

Chapter 6

Twala the Terrible

As we made the journey along the white road, Infadoos told me more of his king. Apparently Twala had killed his twin brother Imotu many years ago in order to seize the throne. Imotu's wife had then fled to the mountains with her infant son, Ignosi, and both were presumed dead.

"If he were still alive, Ignosi would be the rightful ruler of the Kukuanas," declared Infadoos with some feeling. I got the impression he didn't much care for Twala.

After two days, we arrived at Leu, the main settlement of Kukuanaland, which lay at the foot of a large hill. Fifty miles or so in the distance, three snow-capped mountains towered over the hundreds of dwellings.

"It's said that those mountains once brought wise men of old to our country," said Infadoos. "Now our kings are buried there, in the Place of Death."

"That must be the site of King Solomon's Mines," I whispered to Sir Henry and the others, recalling the map.

We were led into the heart of the settlement and made comfortable in a large hut. After we had eaten, Umbopa inquired about Sir Henry's brother, but sadly met with no success.

"Perhaps he never got here?" suggested Good. "We only discovered it by a miracle."

"I don't know," said Sir Henry thoughtfully. "But somehow I'm sure I'll find him."

Presently, Infadoos returned to say that Twala was ready to meet us. We followed him to the heart of the settlement, and were seated before a massive hut. Around it stood thousands of warriors, all as still as statues.

The hut door opened, and a gigantic cloaked figure emerged. His cruel-looking face was made even more terrifying by the fact that he had just one gleaming black eye.

This giant was joined by Scragga, and what at first appeared to be a withered-up monkey, wrapped in a fur cape.

"Be humble, oh people," piped this creature in a thin voice, "it is the King."

"It is the King," boomed out the thousands of warriors in answer.

Silence followed, broken only by the clatter of a spear falling to the ground.

Twala cast his single eye in the direction of the warrior who had dropped his weapon.

"Would you make your King look foolish in front of these strangers from the stars?" he snapped.

The King nodded to Scragga, who gave an an ugly grin. Next second, a spear flew from the youth's hand and went hurtling clean through the unfortunate soldier.

I could see that Sir Henry was boiling with rage at what had just happened.

"Keep quiet, for heaven's sake," I whispered to him. "Our lives depend on it."

Twala turned to us. "Should I do the same to you?" he asked, threateningly.

"Touch one hair of our heads and destruction shall come upon you," I said, as firmly as I could under the circumstances.

Taking up my rifle, I fired a shot at the spear, causing the blade to shatter.

At this, the monkey-like attendant threw off its cloak to reveal a body that resembled a withered, sun-dried corpse. She placed a skinny claw on Twala's shoulder and fixed her beady black eyes on us.

"What seek you, white men of the stars?" she croaked. "Do you seek a lost one... or bright stones? You shall not find them here."

Then she turned her bald vulture-head towards Umbopa. "And what do you seek?" she sneered. "Ha! I think I know."

She raised her skeletal arms skyward. "Blood, blood, blood!" she screeched. "There will be rivers of blood, I foretell it!"

Chapter 7

Umbopa's secret

We returned to our hut, and after a brief discussion with Sir Henry and Good, I shared our thoughts with Infadoos.

"We feel that Twala is a cruel king," I said.

"It's true, my lords," sighed the old warrior. "The land cries out with his cruelties. The innocent die, just for his pleasure. And if Twala fears a man, he will make Gagool smell that man out as a wizard, and he will be killed."

"Why do your people not rise up against him?" asked Sir Henry.

"Then Scragga would reign in his place," replied Infadoos, "and the heart of Scragga is blacker than the heart of Twala. If only Ignosi had lived..."

"I did," said Umbopa.

We all looked in amazement at the man.

"I am Ignosi, rightful King of the Kukuanas," he declared proudly.

"How can that be?" asked Infadoos.

"After my father Imotu was killed by Twala, my mother and I joined a wandering tribe, till at length she died. I carried on alone, until I reached the north and lived among the white men. But I always knew I would return to my own people one day."

"So that's why you joined our expedition," said Good.

Infadoos was not yet convinced. "If you are truly the son of Imotu, you will bear the mark of the great snake," he said.

With that, Umbopa lifted his shirt to reveal a magnificent deep blue tattoo of a snake, coiled dramatically around his waist.

Infadoos fell upon his knees. "It's the King!"

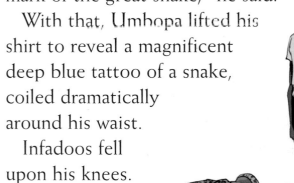

"Rise," said Umbopa. "I am not yet King, but with your help, and that of these brave white men, I shall be."

We began to make plans. There was to be a great dance for our benefit tomorrow. Infadoos would use this distraction to round up the local chiefs on the nearby hill and persuade them to join Umbopa's cause. We were to join him there after the dancing.

The next afternoon, we were brought before Twala once more. This time, the warriors had been replaced by beautiful girls.

"Let the dance begin," cried Twala.

At this, the girls began whirling around and around, singing a sweet song.

One by one, they pirouetted in front of us with the grace of the greatest ballet dancers.

"Which is the prettiest, white men?" asked Twala as the dancing ended.

"The first," I replied, without thinking.

"Then she must die!" announced Twala. "Scragga, make sharp your spear."

Umbopa strode up to Twala defiantly. "I will kill you before you kill this girl."

Twala looked shocked. "Who are you to challenge Twala the Terrible?"

Umbopa's chest swelled with pride. "I am Ignosi, true King of the Kukuanas!"

Undaunted, Scragga raised his weapon.

"Stop!" cried Sir Henry, rushing forward to the bloodthirsty youth.

Animated by fear or fury, Scragga drove his spear with all his force at Sir Henry's broad chest. With an agility for which I would not have given him credit, Sir Henry dodged the blow with a whisker to spare.

Before Scragga had time to strike again, Sir Henry snatched up the spear and sent it straight through his attacker.

At this, the dancing girls ran off in all directions, screeching in panic, and we took the opportunity to make good our escape.

Chapter 8

The battle for Kukuanaland

When we reached the hill, we found Infadoos had not been idle. Thousands of warriors were converging on the summit.

The chiefs were called for and Umbopa, or rather Ignosi, told his story once more. Soon they bowed down before him, just as Infadoos had done.

"It's done," announced Infadoos calmly. "Now we must prepare to fight."

It became clear that Twala's forces had the same idea. From our vantage point we could make out small groups scuttling to and fro from the main settlement in search of reinforcements.

"They won't attack until darkness has passed," said Ignosi. "We must make ready."

As dawn approached, Ignosi gave us our orders. Sir Henry, along with Infadoos and his regiment of old warriors known as the Greys, would attack the front of Twala's column. A group led by Ignosi and myself would then back them up. Meanwhile Good would join the attack on Twala's right flank, and another group would engage the left.

We had brought our rifles with us, but scarcity of ammunition, coupled with the sheer numbers of troops amassed against us, meant they were next to useless. So we armed ourselves with spears, fearsome looking knives and hide-covered iron shields.

As we went to our posts, we wished each other luck, though I doubted whether any of us would live to see the sunset.

Taking my position with Ignosi, I watched anxiously as Twala's troops stormed out of the settlement, and the Greys surged down the hillside to confront them.

Soon the two sides became entangled amid the clashing of shields, spears and knives.

For what seemed an eternity, the battle raged on, until it became clear that the Greys had the upper hand. They overran their opponents and took up a defensive position on a raised knoll, halfway between our hill and the main settlement.

Then Ignosi raised his spear above his head, gave the piercing Kukuana battle cry, and we charged down the hill to join our allies.

I can recall little of what happened next, save that I seemed to get caught up in a sea of warriors.

The next thing I knew, I found myself deposited, battered and bruised, at Sir Henry's feet atop the knoll. But my relief at finding my friend alive was tempered by the sight of Twala's men surging forward.

Again and again, they attacked. Again and again, we beat them back.

Suddenly, Twala himself emerged from the ranks and lashed out at Sir Henry with his fearsome weapon, catching him a fearful blow on the face. Blood poured from the wound.

My friend staggered back, and I feared he was done for, as Twala threw himself at Sir Henry in a fresh assault.

Sir Henry's mighty hand gripped Twala's muscular arm to prevent him landing a fatal blow. Somehow the weapon was wrested from the King's grasp, and the next second Sir Henry swung it around his head, before hitting his opponent with all his force. There was a shriek of horror from a thousand throats, as Twala's head sprang from his shoulders and fell at Ignosi's feet.

At that moment, a deafening battle cry filled the air, and the two remaining regiments, with Captain Good somewhere among them, swarmed down to trap our enemy in a pincer movement.

The opposing forces engaged, but Twala's men had lost the will to put up a struggle. In just five minutes, the fate of the battle was decided. My friends and I stood in silence, exhausted.

Around us, the dead and the dying lay in heaped-up masses. It had come at a price, but Twala the Terrible's reign was at an end.

Chapter 9

King Solomon's Mines

It was several days before any of us were fit enough to turn our attention to the original objective of our expedition.

Sir Henry still believed there was a chance that his brother had made it to the mines.

He had no interest in their content however, agreeing that Good and I should divide any spoils between us. I rather felt that a share of the fabled diamonds would be just compensation for what we'd all been through.

Now formally crowned king, Ignosi ordered Gagool to guide us to The Three Witches. This was the local name for the imposing triangle of mountains which we'd seen on our arrival.

So it was that, early one morning, and with ill-concealed hostility, Gagool led Sir Henry, Good, Infadoos and myself along the final stretch of the great white road.

Three days later, we reached the foot of the mountains, where we came upon the first of many breathtaking sights. Before us was a massive hole in the earth, some three hundred feet deep and about half a mile across.

"This must be the mine," I exclaimed in awe. All around the rim I could see areas that had been levelled out, in order to wash the stones. But, search as we might, there was no sign of the gemstones themselves.

We marched on, and circled the pit until we rejoined the road. It was early evening when we first made out three towering shapes at the foot of the mountains. As we got nearer, I realized that they were magnificent statues, carved out of the rock.

"Behold the Silent Ones," said Infadoos reverently.

"I think they must be ancient gods, conceived by some Phoenician architect, I shouldn't wonder," suggested Sir Henry.

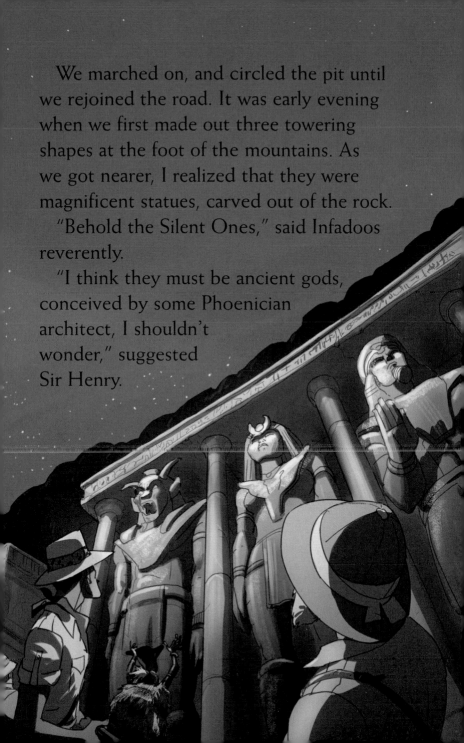

Passing by the statues, Gagool led us to an arched portal in the rockface.

"Now, white men from the stars," she said with a wicked grin, "are you ready? I must obey my king and show you the store of bright stones."

Sir Henry, Good and I nodded. But as we made to go inside, Infadoos hung back.

"It's not for me to enter there," he said with a frown, clearly bound by some age-old law. "But be warned, Gagool. If harm comes to my lords, you shall die."

Our way lit by a gourd of oil carried by the old witch, we walked along the narrow passage until at last we emerged into a vast, cathedral-like cave.

The place must have been a hundred feet high, dimly lit from above somehow, and was lined with shining white stalactites that resembled giant pillars of ice. I could have spent many hours examining this wondrous sight, but Gagool was eager to get her business over.

She led us to the top of the cave, through a doorway and along another passage which emerged into a much smaller chamber.

As Gagool's evil chuckle echoed around us, I stood transfixed by its grisly contents. They will remain engraved on my mind till the day I die.

Chapter 10

The Place of Death

Towering over the room was a massive human skeleton. It was carved out of white stalactite, which gave it an eerie luminescence. In its hand was a spear. But this bizarre spectacle was not the worst of it. Sat on a low stone table was the body of King Twala, his head resting upon his knees.

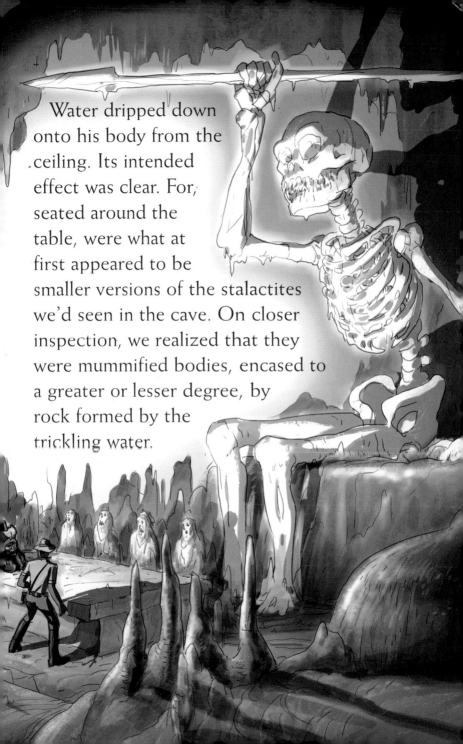

Water dripped down onto his body from the ceiling. Its intended effect was clear. For, seated around the table, were what at first appeared to be smaller versions of the stalactites we'd seen in the cave. On closer inspection, we realized that they were mummified bodies, encased to a greater or lesser degree, by rock formed by the trickling water.

"You know who they are, of course?" whispered Good after a time.

"The former rulers of Kukuanaland, I fear," replied Sir Henry. "Petrified, one and all."

"What a ghastly way to bury the dead," said Good.

"Now Gagool," I said in a low voice, "lead us to the treasure chamber."

Gagool hobbled into the shadows to a featureless wall behind the skeleton. "Here is the chamber, my lords."

"Don't jest with us," I said sternly, surveying the flat, solid rock.

"I do not jest," she cried. "See!"

At that instant, a mass of stone slowly rose from the floor and disappeared into the rock immediately above.

I guessed that Gagool had operated some secret lever, though she had been careful to avoid us seeing it.

We made our way down the dim tunnel, at the end of which stood an elaborately carved wooden doorway.

At last we stood on the threshold of the treasure room.

"Enter my lords," rasped Gagool. "But be warned, there is a saying that those who enter there will die within a moon!"

"Oh confound it all," said Good, grabbing Gagool's lamp and shoving open the door. "I'm not going to be frightened by her."

"Let my lords look for a nook," said Gagool, as we entered the small room. "In the nook you will find what you seek."

After a certain amount of fumbling around in the dark, we located a recess in the wall. Within it sat three stone chests. The lid of one had been removed, and lay resting by its side. Sir Henry held the lamp over it.

"Look!" he gasped.

The chest was piled high with dazzling, uncut diamonds, most of them a considerable size. An examination of the other chests revealed much the same.

I stooped and picked up a handful of the stones. "We're the richest men in the whole world," I gasped.

For a minute or so, we stood transfixed by the wealth before us. But our moment of triumph was short lived.

"Hee, hee! Farewell, foolish men from the stars!" came a cry from outside the room.

We ran from the treasure room to find Gagool standing on our side of the stone door, which was rapidly descending.

With a last cackle, she ducked through the decreasing gap leading back to the Place of Death.

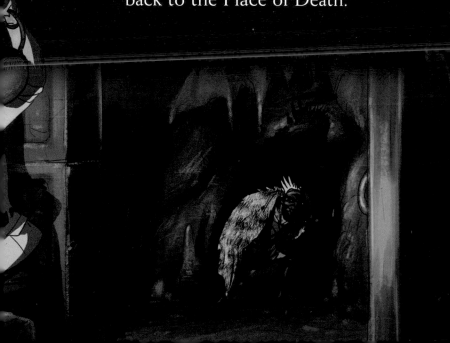

But Gagool had left her escape too late. The thirty ton slab caught her in its vice-like grip, until her body was pressed flat against the rock floor. There was a blood-curdling shriek, followed by a long, sickening crunch, and Gagool the witch was no more.

"Good riddance," I said, unable to feel any pity for such a wicked creature.

"We may soon join her," sighed Sir Henry.

"Eh? What do you mean?" asked Good.

"Don't you see, man?" said Sir Henry gravely. "We're trapped."

Chapter 11

Buried alive

We spent the next hour frantically searching the passageway for a device that might release the door, but to no avail. We concluded that the control must be in the Place of Death. Gagool had operated it, then ducked back into the passageway for a last gloat. This risky act had cost her her life.

Very soon, the oil in the gourd ran out and we found ourselves in total darkness, which only added to the horror of our situation.

We had a small supply of matches, but decided to use them sparingly.

I wondered how long it would take before Infadoos came after us. Days perhaps? But even if he did, would he ever find the secret entrance to our tomb?

Only by our watches could we judge that night had turned to day, and then to night once more.

In the early hours of the morning, a thought suddenly occurred to me.

"How is it that the air keeps fresh?" I asked. "That stone door is air-tight."

"Good heavens, you're right," said Good. "It must come from somewhere. Let's look."

We scrambled around the chamber, feeling for a crack in the rock. At last, Good felt a faint gust of air coming through the floor. He rose and stamped on the place. It rang hollow.

I rubbed my hands over the ground and felt a stone ring, set level with the rock. Heaving with our combined force, we raised the flagstone until, with a rush of air, it fell aside. I lit a match and peered into the hole. I could hardly believe our luck. There were the first steps of a stone staircase.

As we prepared to leave, I couldn't resist pausing to fill every available pocket with diamonds from the chest.

"Won't you fellows take some with you?" I asked, as Good vanished from view.

"Oh, hang the diamonds!" said Sir Henry. "I hope I never see another."

And so we descended.

I counted fifteen steps, which ended in a labyrinth of tunnels. We spent the next few hours groping our way along, most of the time in darkness, hoping the ground beneath our feet wouldn't give way without warning.

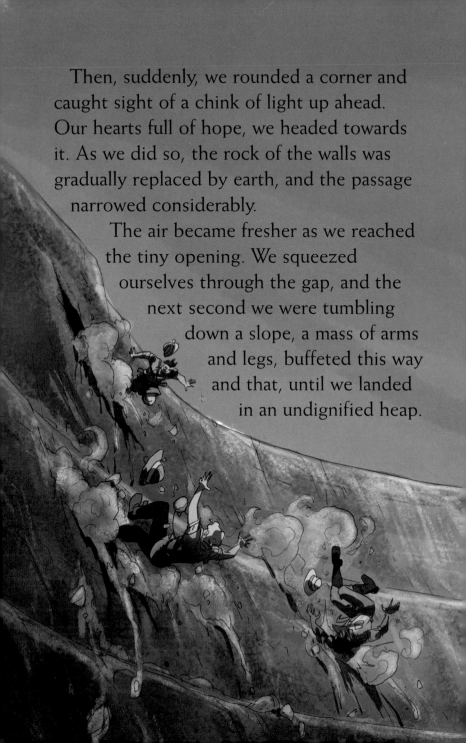

Then, suddenly, we rounded a corner and caught sight of a chink of light up ahead. Our hearts full of hope, we headed towards it. As we did so, the rock of the walls was gradually replaced by earth, and the passage narrowed considerably.

The air became fresher as we reached the tiny opening. We squeezed ourselves through the gap, and the next second we were tumbling down a slope, a mass of arms and legs, buffeted this way and that, until we landed in an undignified heap.

We struggled to our feet and took in our surroundings.

"It's the pit!" cried Sir Henry.

Sure enough, we had emerged at the bottom of the mine workings we had seen on our arrival at The Three Witches. It seemed like a lifetime ago.

Somehow we found the strength to scale the side of the crater, until at last we reached ground level once more.

As we did so, a familiar figure rushed along the road towards us.

"Oh my lords!" cried Infadoos. "It is indeed you, come back from the dead!"

The old warrior flung himself at our feet and wept with joy.

Chapter 12

A final surprise

When we returned to Leu, Ignosi made many generous offers to us to stay, but we were all eager to get home. My only regret was that we had not been successful in our original objective. I could see the sadness in Sir Henry's eyes as we left the settlement, surrounded as we were by hundreds of cheering Kukuanas.

Infadoos told us of another route to the desert, just north of Sheba's Peaks, which was considerably quicker and less hazardous than the one we had taken. The old warrior came with us as far as he could, then bade us a tearful farewell.

Three days later, we had left that wonderful hidden land behind us and were well across the desert. It was then that something quite extraordinary occurred.

As we approached an oasis to fill our water bottles, a curious sight met our eyes. Not twenty yards ahead was a small hut.

At that moment a tanned man, with a big black beard and clad in skins, emerged from the hut. He seemed to be lame, and as he hobbled towards us, he gave a cry. When he got closer, he exchanged looks with Sir Henry and then collapsed in a sort of faint.

"Great powers!" cried Sir Henry. "It's my brother George!"

Presently George recovered, and he and his brother hugged each other with joy. Whatever they had argued about in the past, it was evidently forgotten now.

We were joined by Jim, the guide to whom I had given directions to the mines all those years ago. He told us how he'd lost the note, and that he and Sir Henry's brother had taken an alternate route.

It was while resting at this oasis that George had met with an accident, when a boulder became dislodged and landed on his leg.

Unable to walk any distance, he'd remained here with his faithful servant ever since. The oasis had provided their water, and the animals that frequented it, their food.

That night we joined George and Jim around a campfire and recounted our own adventures.

"By Jove, Henry," said George, when we had shown him the diamonds, "at least you have got something to show for your pains, besides my worthless self."

"They belong to Quatermain and Good," laughed Sir Henry. "It was part of the bargain that they should share any spoils."

Good and I later tried to persuade Sir Henry to take a third share, but he'd have none of it. So, with his consent, we agreed to give them to his brother, who'd suffered as much as we had in the search for treasure.

Our journey back to Sitanda's Kraal was an arduous one, especially as we had to support George. But somehow we managed it.

Five months later, Sir Henry, George and Captain Good set sail for England, while I returned to my little house in Durban.

Not long ago, I received a letter from Sir Henry, inviting me to stay with him in England for a time, if only to write an account of our amazing adventures.

And do you know, I think I'll take him up on his offer. Somehow it's a task I don't like to entrust to anybody else.

H. Rider Haggard
1856-1925

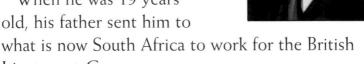

Henry Rider Haggard was born
in Norfolk, England, the eighth
of a family of ten children.

When he was 19 years
old, his father sent him to
what is now South Africa to work for the British
Lieutenant-Governor.

Returning to England in 1882, he studied law,
but he spent most of his time writing novels. His
stories drew on his experiences in Africa, and often
featured intrepid adventurers and lost civilizations.

He wrote *King Solomon's Mines* (1885) after one of
his brothers made him a bet that he couldn't write
a story as good as Robert Louis Stevenson's *Treasure
Island* (1883). Haggard's novel was a huge hit.

As well as writing, he toured the world advising
on agriculture and land use. He was made a Knight
Commander of the British Empire in 1919.

Haggard died in London in 1925, aged 68.

Series editor: Lesley Sims

First published in 2012 by Usborne Publishing Ltd., Usborne House, 83-85 Saffron
Hill, London EC1N 8RT, England. www.usborne.com Copyright © 2012 Usborne
Publishing Ltd. All rights reserved. No part of this publication may be reproduced,
stored in a retrieval system or transmitted in any form or by any means, electronic,
mechanical, photocopying, recording or otherwise, without the prior permission of
the publisher. The name Usborne and the devices 🔔⊕ are Trade Marks of Usborne
Publishing Ltd. UE. First published in America in 2012.